The Days of Joseph
Mahanaim

JOHN NOBLE

For Rachel, the little one in the family who always wears a
smile

Contents

Chapter 1

Messengers

"Joseph, get up." His mother's urgent voice cut straight into a dream of talking sheep.

"What…?" the young boy groaned, rolled over and pulled the wool blanket tight against the cool night air. His eyes peeked open to find his mom, Rachel, bustling about their small tent.

Holding a lit oil lamp in one hand, she rapidly gathered the three clay pots they'd unpacked that evening. As he watched, she hurriedly wrapped each in protective cloth then proceeded to stack them, one inside the next.

Drifting through the tent flap from outside came more noises. Joseph caught the baying of animals being roused from their sleep, mingled with the shouts of servants. All of it confused, sharp – frantic.

Joseph stared blankly, his drowsy mind trying to piece everything together, even as a knot of cold fear puddled in his stomach. Mom seemed… worried… really worried, her hands fumbled with the knots as she bundled their cookware back into the camel's saddlebags. She glanced over, eyes narrowing at seeing him still lying on his bed mat. "Joseph, I said get up."

"Alright, alright." He yawned and massaged his forehead with both hands, before sitting up. "What's happening?"

"We're leaving," she answered, her voice strained, like there was a lot more to it than just that. "Your father is…"

She didn't finish, but Joseph could fill in what she meant. Mom acted like he was too little to understand, but he knew enough. Dread nipped at him as it sank in. They were running… again, weren't they? Joseph couldn't stop a sigh that slipped out. They'd been running for almost two weeks, ever since Harran, and he'd hoped maybe they were at the end. Apparently not.

"They're moving the animals across the river," his mom added as she briskly folded a blanket.

Joseph blinked, certain he'd misheard. "Tonight?" Hadn't they just finished doing that? He'd spent half the day helping Dad and the servants split out five smaller herds, which they'd driven across the river and ahead to Uncle Esau. Now suddenly Dad wanted to do it again, with *all* the animals, *at night*?

For a few heartbeats, Joseph stared, wondering if this was just an awful dream. But Mom still bustled around the tent, and now that he listened, he could catch the mingled whoops and hollers of his brothers and the servants herding the livestock.

Frustrated, and stifling another yawn, Joseph rose and donned his tan work tunic. Peering out from the tent flap, he was met with a dark world bathed in cold starlight.

Then his eyes focused, and his breath drew sharp.

The warriors. From Mahanaim.

They were here.

His family had camped in a vale by the river crossing. In the daylight, low hills had been visible rising up to either side and shielding them from the worst of the crisp night breeze. But now those same rises were lined with… Messengers, his dad had called them. They were tall men, clothed in blinding white tunics and wearing golden armor that glowed like brilliant stars in the darkness.

They had formed a loose, half-circle cordon around the camp. Now they stood in pairs, back-to-back. One seemingly kept watch over their camp, while the other stared out into the utter darkness of the night. Even from a distance, Joseph could pick out their weapons glowing with embers of golden fire in the blackness. Each carried a mighty, two-handed sword that gleamed of polished golden bronze, and which at five, Joseph could only dream of lifting.

The Messengers weren't advancing though. Instead, they stood there just watching… waiting, their blades unsheathed and the points casually sunk into the earth, ready but strangely at ease. The Messenger's formation was unmistakable. The twelve pairs of men had spread in a crescent around their camp, pinning them against the river. Gazing a moment, mouth agape, Joseph finally stepped back inside. He let the tent flap drop, abruptly cutting off the chilly air oozing in.

"Mom, what do they want?"

His mother hesitated. "I think…" for an instant Joseph hoped she might explain what was going on, but finally she just shook her head. "I don't know. Your father thinks they want us to leave, to keep moving."

Joseph was only five, but even he frowned at that. Leave? Right now? That didn't make any sense. He'd fallen asleep listening to his mom, Aunt Leah and dad sitting outside the tent, whispering in hushed voices. Whispering about the uncle he'd never met, who seemed to have even his dad scared. He still remembered Dad's quiet tone before drifting off, "When he comes tomorrow, we keep the river between him and us."

"And if he tries to cross?" Leah's matter-of-fact voice was laced with worry. "They said your brother had an army."

"I've already talked with Nashu and Bariel," his dad said flatly. "If it comes to blows, they'll lead the servants to hold the ford as long as they can. You and Rachel just get the children and get away. Get back to Harran. Leave the animals… all of it. Just save who you can and go. Promise me."

Both women hesitated and Rachel finally asked, "What about you?"

For a long moment his dad didn't answer. "Promise me," he finally said, "promise you'll run."

"Jacob, we can't just–"

"Promise me."

"Promise me."

Back in the chaotic present, Joseph turned at the swish of the tent flap to see his father stoop inside. "Rachel, we need to..." his voice trailed off at seeing Joseph still there.

When he spoke again, his father's voice was curt, Dad's usual friendliness stolen away. "Joseph, they need you down by the river to help move the goats."

Joseph's face fell at the news. "The goats?" The goats were about the worst of the animals to get stuck with, ornery, stubborn and entirely too eager to snap a back leg into your gut faster than you could blink.

"Go." Dad held open the tent flap with one arm and nodded for Joseph to leave, his expression the stern sort that wouldn't accept any argument.

"But, Dad, why are–"

"Go."

Joseph looked at his mother, except she didn't seem like she'd support him either.

Grabbing his stick from the corner, Joseph let out a frustrated sigh, ducked beneath the tent flap and hurried outside. What he found was a camp in uproar. Splashes of torchlight weaved in and out of tents, and the shouts drowned one another in a jumbled chaos. Somewhere close by, a camel's loud *Mwwaaatt* groan cut through it all.

He could dimly hear the cacophony of animal sounds coming from down by the river, mingled with aggressive shouts and bobbing puddles of light that signaled his brothers.

Searching ahead with his stick, Joseph made it all of ten steps in the moonless night before his foot caught a stone. He gasped as a jolt of pain stabbed his big toe. Clutching it with a hiss, he hopped twice before the pain dimmed enough to lower his foot and steady himself.

In the gloom, his eyes were drawn back towards the Messengers, standing like blazing statues atop the hills. He stared until more shouts snapped him out of his vigil, and he set off at a cautious jog towards the commotion down at the river. Even so, he chanced a quick look back at the Messengers, still watching… waiting… but for what?

***

"Joseph! Are you stupid? I said keep left!" Reuben loomed up out of the chaotic, noise-torn night. He held a torch glowing with orange flames in one hand and his staff in the other.

In front of them, the goats milled about in a tight, bleating bunch. The flock was pressing down a short slope against the rocky north bank of the Jabbok River. They'd crowded down close to the ford, but none seemed brave enough to tread through the dark, knee-deep water.

Joseph hesitated at Reuben's order. His eyes darted left to another pool of flickering orange light where he could see his older brother, Simeon, busy berating Gad and Asher for being slow. He wasn't *stupid*, he'd just really rather *not* be over there.

5

He turned back to Reuben, "Why do we have to do this tonight, can't we–"

He didn't get to finish. Three rams had circulated to the front of the herd. Stamping at the slope, they abruptly made a charge to breakout of the cordon of eleven boys pinning them against the water.

Reuben screamed, a noise like a yowling desert lynx. He rushed the goats, his torch trailing sparks as he waved his arms wildly, lashing them with his staff. The rams scattered, two curving right. Joseph knew enough to dart in front of them, waving his own stick to cut them off and screaming, *"Hê-aaaa!* Get back!'

The two rams hesitated a heartbeat, angling like they might just try to take him on. Joseph wasn't very big, and the rams probably outweighed him. If they charged, he knew it was get out of the way or get run over.

Joseph didn't hesitate though. He rushed at the goats shouting like his brothers and twirling his stick like he'd seen the caravan guards do with their spears in Harran. For a half second, he was certain they'd charge him anyway. But then the goats veered off and plunged back to the safety of the herd that swirled in front of them.

Reuben was already screaming more orders as he ran to circle around the last stray goat. It had stopped and was glancing back at the herd like he wanted the rest of his friends to follow. "Dan, watch those three! Levi, close in on the right!"

In a minute, Reuben had the final goat driven back to the shoreline. Joseph saw his oldest brother pause, glancing around and taking in the absolute mess of a midnight adventure. More frantic shouts echoed nearby, and Joseph wilted at the way Reuben's brow furled when the older boy's eyes finally swept around to him.

"I said get over and help Simeon," Reuben snapped.

"But why–"

"Look, I don't know why Dad decided the middle of the night was a good time for this," Reuben's biting sarcasm mostly hid the worried edge in his voice. "We have to get them moving though and…"

Reuben's voice trailed off and he shook his head, frustration boiling out as he swiped his staff at the air. Joseph wasn't sure what to make of Reuben's indecision. Mostly he just tried *not* to be in his older brother's line of sight.

Finally, Reuben sighed and jammed the bottom end of his stick into the dirt, leaning on his staff as he stared off to the right. "You know what," Reuben said, "scratch that about helping Simeon. Go right, and tell Levi to get into the herd and grab one of the goats. It doesn't really matter which one. Just have him get one and drag it across the river. That might start the rest of them moving."

Joseph gulped, still uncertain. It wasn't that it was a bad plan just, "I'm not sure if Levi will take orders from–"

"He's not taking orders from *you*," Reuben snapped, a dark frown creasing his face. "We don't have time for this *khará*. If Levi wants to throw a fit, I'll come over there and beat him myself. Now get moving before the herd decides to scatter and we have to spend the rest of the night chasing them down."

Reuben clipped Joseph with his staff. His way of saying goodbye, and Joseph stumbled away a few steps, rubbing his smarting shoulder, but wise enough not to complain. He tried to recall the ford as he had seen it earlier that day and broke into a jog. It was a fight not to stumble in the darkness as he made a wide arc around the herd of goats, aiming to link up with Levi. He took a deliberately long route, making sure not to move too close and spook the animals. A wild rush of panicked goats was the last thing they needed right now. Pinned as the animals were, pressuring them could end like sitting on an old water skin. If squeezed too hard, they'd panic and break out in a wild flood that none of them would be able to stop.

He glanced back at the rapidly moving pinpricks of light in camp, then to the hills beyond where the Messengers still hadn't moved from their vigil. He wished they could have shown up four hours ago. The herds they'd pushed over the river earlier that day hadn't made much of a fuss. But that had been with the sun high overhead, so they could see where they were going. Now, trying to get them to splash through the river in the darkness seemed like trying to roll a boulder uphill.

He found Levi grumpy, as expected. The older boy was guarding the right flank of the herd with Issachar and Zebulun, screaming at the 'stupid animals', his 'stupid brothers', and this 'stupid plan' all in no particular order.

"I said *fan out*!" Levi shouted at the two boys, neither much older than Joseph. He swept his torch in a wide arc with a sarcastic, "FAN OUT! Can you two not grasp what that means?"

"Levi…"

The older boy wheeled on Joseph, his exasperation boiling over like porridge left too long on the coals. "What do you want, *Tiny*?"

Joseph gulped. He didn't like that name. It never felt like anyone meant it nice.

"Reuben wants you to get one of the goats and drag it across," the words spilled out between breaths. "He sent me to tell you."

For a heartbeat, Levi glared at him in disbelief. "*Sure*," he finally said with a sarcastic nod, "Just let me go find my magic flying sandals and I'll get right on that."

"Levi–"

But his older brother wasn't listening. "Zebulun," he waved his brother further left, "don't let them push up along the bank!"

When he turned back to Joseph, Levi was glowering and mumbling to himself, "Maybe Reuben could go do his own dirty work for once."

He whacked at a loose pebble with the end of his staff, sending it skittering down the ford toward the pitch-black waters. Levi turned away, muttering in an angry, sullen tone. All Joseph caught were the words 'lazy' and 'useless' — enough to make him keep a safe distance in case Levi decided to whack something else.

This was how things always were. As the oldest, Reuben should have had Simeon, the second oldest, grab the goat. Simeon was bigger, stronger, and could wrestle one of the feisty animals much better than Levi, who was a full year younger. But, of course, if Reuben tried to tell Simeon to do *anything,* Simeon would say *No* and there'd be a huge fight. By the time they settled on *who* could make *whom* do *what,* the goats would be long gone. Meanwhile the Messengers up in the hills would be… who knew.

A few goats made tepid steps towards Levi, and he slashed his torch through the air with an angry shout to drive them back. Finally, he turned to Joseph, still mumbling and with a scowl on his face. "Fine," he grumbled, "So long as Reuben knows this is going to be a complete disaster."

Joseph didn't answer.

Fortunately, Levi didn't seem to care. "Take this, and hold here, Joseph." Levi shoved his torch into the boy's hand, even as he began snapping orders. "Issachar, Zebulun," he shouted to the boys on either side, "Remember, arms wide, look big! Things are about to get interesting!"

Joseph gulped back his nervousness. He held his staff out wide and the flaming torch high, trying not to

look as vulnerable as he felt. For his part, Levi took a
deep breath, and rushed straight into the center of the
writhing pack of animals.

Joseph could swear the herd was a living creature,
shifting and flowing like a school of fish in a pond. It
opened for Levi, then swept closed behind him, the
goats all jockeying to keep at a distance.

Joseph's eyes were partially blinded by the torch
which cast back the night, and Levi mostly vanished
into the murky gloom. Joseph could still hear his older
half-brother's shouts drifting across the cacophony of
bleating goats. "You owe me big for this one,
Reuben!" Then the sharp crack of wood on a goat's
bony rear, "Move, you worthless… HA, got you! Stop
squirming and go!" A moment's break then, "It's just
water, COME ON!"

He heard a distressed '*MAHAAAAA*' over it all, and
the herd seemed to surge in every direction at once.
Joseph fought back a stab of panic as it seemed like
every single goat stood on the cusp of charging
outwards. Panicked rams stamped at the pebble
shoreline and several started straight towards him.

Joseph fought back the fear and screamed. Not a
scared yell, but a loud, *don't mess with me* shout. For
an instant, he felt almost like Dad. He spread his arms
wide and swept the torch in front of him. Sparks
trailed in the night, and nearby he heard his other
brothers shouting, all of them in unison.

The flock wilted in terror under their cries. Joseph
took a single step forward and all the resistance
abruptly gave way. Where before there had been a
packed mass of animals, now the swirling herd
receded down the slope to the riverbank. He heard a
chorus of discordant splashes in the dark river. From
down in the water came Levi's excited shout, "They're
coming!"

Joseph took a deep breath and let out a relieved
sigh. He held his torch high as they chased the last of

the goats into the river, halting at the bank. For once they were all in a good, or at least *relieved* mood. Even Reuben and Simeon looked like they weren't about to pound each other.

Scrambling back up the gentle slope, Joseph turned and saw that the rest of the camp appeared to be moving towards them, donkeys packed and tents dismantled. They were all heading towards the river, but behind them someone else was coming too.

The Messengers, they were moving… following.

Chapter 2

The Struggle

Joseph tested the pitch-black water, dipping a single sandaled foot into the river. The liquid felt like ice on his toes, and he pulled away, kicking the air to flick off a few drops.

Reuben and Simeon had both immediately waded across after the goats, but Simeon had slipped, gone under and nearly pulled Reuben and his torch down as well. Both boys had come out shivering and soaked on the other side after struggling through the current.

As the youngest of his brothers, Joseph didn't like his chances crossing on his own. If he slipped in the pale starlight, he'd be lucky to *only* end up choking down a mouthful of river water. Assuming he came back up at all.

So Joseph waited, anxiously kicking pebbles as the long caravan of camels trudged up, burdened down with all the camp gear.

His dad was in the front, pulling along a stubborn camel by the halter, while his mom sat in the saddle. A train of servants behind led on more of the plodding creatures. "Dad," Joseph jogged up as they came close, "what's going on?"

Joseph had hoped for a real answer, but as he drew near, his parents broke off whatever they'd been talking about. His mom didn't look happy, but his dad forced a tentative smile, obviously worried but doing his best to veil it.

Instead of answering, his father glanced across the river towards the bleating goats. "You got the herd across?" he asked, his voice big and solemn.

A part of Joseph wanted to know more, but he gave a small nod anyway. His dad's smile widened, more sincere, "Well done." He patted Joseph on the shoulder, and nodded towards the camel, "Hop on. Unless you prefer to swim across."

Joseph liked to think he'd gotten pretty good at riding camels in the last few weeks since leaving Harran. But even so, his first attempt to scramble up the side of his mom's camel ended with his sandal slipping. He dropped back onto the rocky dirt, red-cheeked and nerving himself for another go. Before he could though, strong hands grabbed him around the waist, and he heard his dad's voice, "I've got you."

Joseph almost protested that he could make it, but before he could, Dad lifted him up. His stomach twisted, and for a moment he was almost flying. Finally, his feet touched the saddle, and Mom grabbed his hand, pulling him into her lap until Joseph was perched safely between her and the camel's oversized hump.

When he glanced around, he saw the rest of his brothers scrambling their way onto mounts as well. In less time than it took to shear a sheep, they were moving again. Joseph jostled at each uneven camel step as Dad led them down into the river.

Even despite the rough ride and the cold breeze biting at his cheeks, Joseph found all the exhaustion from when he'd awoken starting to creep back. It was late. He leaned on his mom's chest and yawned as they splashed through the shallows. Joseph glanced back at her, "Mom, are we going to have to unpack everything tonight too?"

Before, her face had seemed serious, but now a hint of a smile crept in. "Not tonight, little one," she said, wrapping a reassuring arm around his chest. "We'll figure it out tomorrow."

Beneath them, the water swished around the camel's legs, drowning them in a murky black that rippled with the reflections of torches. "Dad?" Joseph asked, casting another look back at the Messengers, now down on the lower slopes of the surrounding hills and rapidly closing, "Why are they chasing us?"

For an instant, Dad didn't answer until, "They're not," he said quietly.

"But they—"

"They're not chasing us," Dad said firmly, even as the water around the camel's knees began to drop lower. "We just have to go."

"But why?"

Dad didn't answer, and kept his silence as he led their camel out of the river and up onto the smooth stones of the far bank, where Reuben, Simeon and Levi were also waiting.

For once Dad didn't ask where the goats were, probably wet, cold, miserable and hopefully bedding down somewhere close by. Behind Joseph came more splashes. The boy craned his neck around to see the rest of the camels sloshing their way up the bank, illuminated in puddles of torchlight. Trailing them came a camel carrying Leah with young Dinah seated up in her lap. That was followed by the rest of Dad's wives on their own mounts.

Further back trailed other servants leading long strings of pack donkeys. They'd be loaded down with supplies, tents... all their possessions, broken down, bundled up and tied onto a bunch of baying animals.

"Take these, Rachel." Dad's voice drew Joseph's eyes back around just in time to see Dad pass the reins up to Mom.

"Jacob—"

Dad shook his head, cutting her off and hesitating a second before giving a knowing nod and a terse, "I'll be fine."

Wait, what?

Before Joseph could ask, his father strode off, giving Levi an encouraging pat on the back and nodding to Reuben and Simeon. "You boys did well." The three were still shivering in drenched tunics, but they stood up a little straighter anyway.

Then Dad turned, and without even a pause, trudged back into the swirling river, torch in hand.

Joseph's eyes widened, and he tried to scramble off the camel, only for Mom's arm to cinch him in place. "What's Dad doing?"

"It's alright," Mom whispered.

Was it? Really? Weren't they all rushing over to this side to get away from the Messengers, and now Dad was turning around and going right back?

Joseph wasn't the only confused one. Nearby, Reuben's worried voice shouted, "Dad, where are you going?"

Dan called too, with Dad only giving him and Naphtali a passing nod as he waded into the river.

Mom flicked the reins and brought the camel around. For a moment, they both watched the glow of the bobbing torch that marked his progress. Dad sank up to his knees in the dark current before wading out and up the opposite bank, just as the last of the pack trains splashed by.

For a second, Dad waited. Joseph had the fleeting hope that maybe he'd simply gone back to make sure the rest of the animals made it across. That hope sputtered and died when the last of the donkeys splashed past. Jacob cast one glance back. Then he held out his flickering torch, hesitated a heartbeat, and tossed it into the inky waters.

The light went out, and just like that, Dad was gone... vanished into the night.

And behind him, the Messengers were still coming.

For several heartbeats, Joseph stared, his eyes vainly trying to pierce the darkness. On a normal night, his eyes might have adjusted, and he could have glimpsed Dad in the faint starlight. Unfortunately, as the Messengers drew close, the ethereal brilliance radiating off them blinded him to everything else. The closest of them were nearly to the waterside now, fanning out in a giant ring that faced outwards.

"Mom, what are they..."

He twisted back and his voice trailed off as he caught his mother's face, forlorn and pale, even in the warm torchlight. In an instant though, she had forced it all back, giving an encouraging but hardly believable, "It'll be fine, Joseph."

Overhead, a low crackle of thunder rumbled like a thousand hoofbeats in the sky. Joseph felt Mom's arm tighten around him, even as he looked up in surprise. Where had a storm come from? There hadn't been a cloud in the sky at sunset.

"Come on," Mom whispered, as a cool breeze brushed at them, "let's get a blanket."

Getting down was a challenge given how tall the camel was. But his mom was strong enough to lower him most of the way, letting him drop the last half cubit to the ground before climbing down herself.

She expertly coaxed the camel onto its belly. The animal gave a low, tired sort of bellow, but complied. In a moment Mom had dug a heavy blanket out of the saddlebag. She untangled a couple of dark lumps from the blanket, quickly stuffing them back in the bag. Then she spread out the coarse wool, sitting with her back to the camel and nodding him to her side.

"Come on, Joseph." Mom patted the ground next to her and held up one edge of the blanket. "It'll be okay."

Would it? It didn't feel right. Dad was still on the other side doing... Joseph wasn't even sure. Overhead, another long roll of thunder pulsed with almost a physical force. Shivering in the cold, Joseph slid in next to her beneath the blanket.

After two weeks constantly on the road, Joseph barely even noticed the distinctive camel aroma, but he did appreciate the warmth on his back. Fighting back a yawn, the boy blinked. Mom put a reassuring arm around him, even as she stared across the dark waters where several of the Messengers had walked right up to the bank. There, the glowing figures had finally paused, planting their massive swords in the pebbles along the riverside.

A third deep peal of thunder tolled like a bell, and Joseph's eyes widened as across the river all the Messengers knelt in perfect unison. They all fell to one knee, then just... vanished.

Joseph blinked, frantically scanning the night as the strange radiance surrounding them was quenched like a candle flame. The far side of the river was plunged into utter darkness.

It seemed like the whole world froze. As hard as he stared, his gaze couldn't pierce the veil that shrouded the opposite side of the river. He couldn't see Dad. Finally, Mom gulped and pulled him close, her voice shaky as she repeated, "It'll be okay, Joseph. Try to get some sleep."

Sleeping didn't feel right at all, like he'd be letting Dad down if he looked away, even for an instant. That was easier said than done though. With his back resting against the steady rise-and-fall beat of the camel's breathing, Joseph soon found his eyes growing heavy.

He fought back another yawn.

Shifting to get comfortable and trying to stay awake, Joseph glanced up. He dimly registered that the sky above was littered with twinkling pinpoints of light. That was strange. There were no clouds to blot out the stars, so where had the thunder come from?

For a while, his exhausted gaze traced across the familiar sky, half puzzling about the thunder and half picking out the familiar stars. Dad and Grandpa Laban had showed him some constellations back in Harran. There was Zappu — the Star of Stars. High above that soared The Great Swallow, and near it sat the Twins. Next to them was his favorite, the Loyal Shepherd, a man with a raised staff and a belt of three distinctive stars that made it easy enough to spot. That one always reminded him of Dad.

For a moment, Joseph wondered what it meant that the constellation was still shining... maybe nothing, he thought. But maybe as long as it was up there, Dad was okay, even if he *was* back across the river. Maybe.

Joseph was still wondering when his eyes slowly slipped shut.

Overhead, the stars shone down, twirling in an endless dance, and on the south bank of the Jabbok River, the scattered caravan fell into an uneasy sleep.

Joseph dreamed of the Messengers.

Chapter 3

Mahanaim

Two Days Earlier

"Are we in Canaan yet?" Joseph mumbled, seated in Mom's lap and trying to ignore the jerking camel's gait.

His mother gave an annoyed sigh. "Joseph, I don't know. You'd have to ask your father."

Beneath them, the camel gave another lazy jostle as it plodded along. He was wedged in between the front ridge of the humped camel saddle and Mom, who was holding the reins with one hand while the other arm looped across his chest. Off to the right, the evening sun dipped lower, slow-motion plunging towards the unfamiliar western hills. Joseph leaned back against his mother, closing his eyes and letting his aching feet take a break. They'd been walking pretty much *all day every day* for over a week now, and he really just wanted to sleep.

The camel bounced again, a sharp jolt that knocked him back to reality. Joseph tried to ignore the discomfort, and got all of five more jerking steps before deciding he couldn't. He didn't know how Mom managed, but she seemed able to calmly sit up here for hours, rocking in sync with the camel.

He held out a few more steps, his boredom looming larger until, "Can I get down?"

"Of course."

They'd had a lot of practice in the weeks since leaving Harran. Joseph swung his legs to one side and latched onto his mother's free hand. She leaned over, gently letting him down until, a cubit above the ground, Joseph let go. He smoothly dropped onto a bare patch of dirt between the clumps of tall grass that dotted the valley. Walking alongside the camel, he grabbed his stick from where he'd tied it to the saddle earlier. He gave it an experimental twirl, then he was off.

Even the half-hour break seemed to have done wonders for his feet. Leaving the camel behind, Joseph wandered towards the front of the strung-out caravan. Maybe his dad would know if this was Canaan. The last couple of days the terrain had certainly changed from endless, big-sky flatlands into rolling hills and snaking valleys. Maybe they were already in Canaan.

Joseph found his father walking near the front of the column, right behind the first train of pack donkeys and a herd of lowing cattle. He was deep in conversation with Bariel and Nashu, "... haven't seen any signs of the pride since noon, and only a few roars this morning," Nashu said, as Joseph wandered up behind them.

"You think they gave up the chase?" Dad asked.

"It's been close on three days, and we wounded one of them. The lions had to go back eventually," the older Bariel pointed out.

Dad gave a slow nod. "I suppose we're fortunate that we only lost two ewes. It could have been much worse." He nodded appreciatively, "Well done. Any news from the men we sent ahead?"

Bariel shook his head. "It's a long journey, maybe tomorrow."

For several steps, Dad didn't speak and finally he gave a deep sigh. "Let me know the moment they get back."

"Of course, sir."

Jacob glanced around and abruptly noticed Joseph wandering close behind them. "Joseph," he frowned, "have you been spying on us?"

"Uhhh..." Joseph swallowed back the *Yes* that almost slipped out.

"I'm sure he has," Nashu declared grimly. "I believe we'll have to eliminate him, sir. Would you like me to handle it?"

Whaaaat? Joseph skipped a step at the serious looks he was getting, right before Dad chuckled, and it clicked that they were joking. Dad flicked a hand for Joseph to join him, even as the two huntsmen fell out, back to their own business.

"It's not polite to listen in without announcing yourself," Dad added.

"I'm sorry." Joseph mumbled, not feeling like he'd done anything wrong, but... whatever.

"Is everything alright?" Dad asked.

Joseph nodded. "I was just wondering if this was Canaan?"

"Part of it, yes," Dad said. He pointed west towards the dipping sun. "There's a river that way that splits the land in two. It's much greener on the other side, and if you go another few days past the river, you'll come all the way to the Great Sea."

"The one that goes forever?" Joseph asked, breathless. He'd heard his brothers talk about it before– so much water you couldn't see the other side. And there were ships that rode on the water and dropped off the edge of the world, vanishing into a strange realm of blue and sun and sky.

Dad laughed, "I'm not sure anything can go forever, but they say it goes for days and days to the west."

Joseph was about to ask more when another servant, one of the herdsmen from up ahead, sprinted back to them, running like mad. "Sir," he ground to a halt, gasping, "strange men, just around the next hill. Armed."

Instantly, Dad's good humor vanished. "Joseph, find your mother."

"But—"

"Go!"

Dad spun to his own donkey, grabbing the heavy war bow and quiver tied on the animal. As Joseph turned and sped off, he heard Dad shouting, "Hold the animals here! Bariel, Nashu– get your weapons!"

Mom was back where Joseph had left her, peering quizzically ahead as the caravan awkwardly ground to a stop. She eyed him with a suspicious frown as he ran up, "Joseph, did you do something?"

The five-year-old boy emphatically shook his head, *No*. Not this time. Instead, he pointed, "There are strange men up ahead. Dad went to see who they are."

"Hmmmm," Mom raised a hand to shield her eyes as she stared up the broad valley they'd been traveling. Finally, she gave up with a sigh, and glanced down, offering him a hand up. "Well, come on."

Joseph stared, lost. "Huh?"

"Don't you want to know who they are too?" Mom asked.

Ohhhh, Joseph realized what she meant. Well, in that case...

He jumped, catching Mom's hand and half flew, half scrambled his way into the saddle.

Mom reined the camel to the side with a clicking *tsk tsk*. While everyone else came to a jumbled halt, the two of them slid out of line and kept to their usual plodding pace. Joseph found himself wishing Mom would go faster. Unfortunately, she was his only way of seeing what was happening at all… well, only way that didn't earn him a scolding. Regardless, he knew enough to keep his impatience to himself.

Soon enough they saw the men, and well... yeah, *strange* about summed it up. They wore gleaming armor plates that shone with a golden polish– chest pieces, vambraces, greaves, but oddly no helmets. Fifty paces ahead of the column, five of them were speaking with Dad. It was hard to tell what was happening, but they didn't *look* unfriendly. Their swords were sheathed, and Dad didn't seem poised like he thought there might be a fight. At seeing the men, Mom flicked the reins with a sharp, *"Arhu"* that accelerated the camel to a gentle jog.

They were still halfway there when Dad turned back from the men with the burnished armor. For a second, Joseph thought he might wave them off, but instead his father gestured for them to join him.

The lazy camel slowly settled back into its usual lumbering pace, and as they came near, Dad was smiling. "Rachel, you're here." He expertly grabbed the camel's harness, guiding the beast down onto its belly, where Joseph could simply slide off and onto the ground. Dad offered Mom a hand out of the saddle as she glanced ahead at the five men. "Jacob, what's going on? Are they from your brother?"

"No, not at all." Dad shook his head, excited. They'd come far enough around the next hill to see down the valley beyond. Dad pointed past the men to where a cluster of small linen-white dots stood some ways off in neatly ordered lines.

Joseph had to stare a moment to realize they were tents, but not anything like the ones he was used to. His Mom's tent was a low hung, sprawling structure that could expand into a space big enough for a whole family, so long as you had enough hide and poles to grow it. These tents though were shaped like tiny white mountains, each peaked at the top, just two poles, four pegs in the ground and a white tarp. The sort of thing you could pack in a flash and set up just as quickly.

Mom stared too, and Joseph caught the confused surprise in her eyes. "Jacob, what is this?"

"This is God's camp!" Jacob declared with a sweeping gesture. He nodded to the men, "These are Messengers, from the Lord."

Whaaaaaaat? Joseph watched the men a moment, half puzzling at what that meant, and half gawking at the extraordinary armor they wore. He dimly caught Mom's concerned tone. "You're certain?"

"I've... seen them before," Jacob said. "A very long time ago."

Behind them, a camel gave a tired groan, and Aunt Leah's voice interrupted. "Jacob, what's going on?"

Joseph glanced back to see Leah and his half-sister Dinah riding forward with Reuben, Levi, and Judah following close behind. Back by the main caravan, more of their group were beginning to trickle ahead, everyone's curiosity gradually getting the better of them.

Jacob helped Leah down and gestured them all to follow. "Come on," he said, "we should introduce ourselves."

***

Joseph awoke to a soft *mmahahaha*.

"Go away..." the boy mumbled sleepily, "...I'm tired..."

Something soft and warm brushed his cheek and Joseph's eyes shot open to find...

A goat?

Mmahahaha.

Even in the moonless dark, he could see the vague outline of a small, stick-legged animal about as tall as he was, with two green-blue eyes reflecting starlight. Joseph started at seeing the long goat-face looming right in front of him, but the goat didn't try to run. It hesitated a second, then nuzzled his cheek again.

"What do you want?" Joseph brushed the creature away.

Unsurprisingly, the goat didn't answer.

Next to him, Mom was asleep. Her head drooped forward, while behind him the camel hadn't budged, the huge belly still rising and falling in ceaseless rhythm.

The goat nudged him again. Rubbing his eyes, Joseph pushed off the blanket. Apparently, the creature just didn't want him to sleep.

He could guess what had happened. The goat had probably gotten lost in the chaos of the crossing and spent half the night wandering around trying to find the rest of the flock. It must have eventually concluded that being with people was better than being all alone. Oh well, he sighed, better here than in a lion's belly.

It was still dark, but overhead a thick band of stars streaked the sky, drenching the world in a pale glow. At five years old, Joseph wasn't that much taller than the goats, but standing, he was surprised to discover more than just one goat there... a lot more.

After the goats had crossed the river, there hadn't been anyone on the other side to round them up, and nowhere to corral them anyway. The entire flock had more or less run off.

Now though, Joseph looked out and saw most of the flock scattered across the dark grass in front of him, just... waiting.

Well, at least that was some good news. He'd been quietly dreading the morning. They could have easily spent half a day rounding up the goats, only to still have a couple of stray bunches scattered about. Unless, of course, they all just came right back.

The first goat, who seemed the most adventurous of the bunch, took a few cautious steps away when Joseph stood, but he didn't run. A good sign.

For a couple moments, Joseph wasn't sure what to do. He didn't want to spook them again. If he'd known where Reuben and Levi were sleeping, he would have gone to bother them, but glancing around, he could only dimly see other camels and clumps of people scattered everywhere. Reuben could be any of them, and waking the wrong people... especially Simeon... that wouldn't go over well.

The goat nudged its head against Joseph once again and the young boy let out a groan. What did it want?

Walking around the flock, he briefly tried to get a count on the animals. But he quickly realized he wasn't tall enough to get a good vantage, and in the night the herd seemed like one dark mass anyway.

But he did notice something odd. He and Mom had bedded down close to the ford, the place where the ground sloped down to meet the rippling water. Off to either side, the sharp banks rose up to become steep cliffs, and they'd spent most of yesterday rotating the herds down to water at the narrow ford. Now though, the goats were all bunched up on the slope that led into to the rippling black waters. They were clustered like they *really* wanted to head down to the river, but part way down the slope the flock abruptly stopped, fanning out like some invisible wall held them back.

Joseph cocked his head, staring a moment and blinking. That was... weird.

The goat moved close and nudged Joseph yet again. The boy glanced at it, then the flock, then down to the river.

Were they... afraid? They wanted water but were too scared to go down?

Grabbing his stick, Joseph peered through the night to the opposite bank, a part of him hoping to see Dad. But even with his eyes adjusted to the dark, he could barely see anything at all. In the dim light, the wide valley opposite him seemed nothing more than mounds of shadow. Eventually, Joseph puffed out a nervous breath... it didn't *look* scary.

The flock seemed to melt away in front of him, goats pressing aside of their own accord to create a path as Joseph crept towards the ford. About a quarter of the way down the bank, Joseph reached the spot where the goats had strangely stopped. Instead of moving further, a line of them now stared longingly towards the river. The symmetric ranks flowed aside as he strolled up, and Joseph hesitated, not sure what was so special about this particular spot. Reaching over the invisible line with his stick, he waved it around a moment.

Seemed fine.

Nothing stirred below along the riverbank, and he glanced back at the goats. What was their problem?

Taking a cautious step across the line, Joseph paused, warily looking around.

Nothing happened.

Glancing back east, he caught the first scarlet-purple brushes of dawn painting across a few thin clouds on the horizon. The image seemed to settle things in Joseph's mind. The goats couldn't just wait around being scared all day. No matter where Dad was, this was still an important day. Uncle Esau was coming with like... an army or something. Now that he thought about it, that didn't exactly sound like good news. Maybe that was what had everyone so worried. Either way, the goats ought to at least drink. They might not have time later.

Feeling ahead with his stick, Joseph cautiously poked his way down to the ford. Overhead, more streaks of dawn blossomed out across the sky, slowly shoving back the night.

Part way down to the river, he looked back and frowned. "Come on," he hissed, gesturing with his staff for the goats to follow. "It's fine."

They'd just resumed their odd line and were staring... at him... past him?

Joseph's gaze roved back across the far bank, bewildered. There was *nothing* there. Exasperated, he wandered the last dozen steps and paused at the edge of the rippling waters now reflecting the gradually brightening sky. Just to make a point, Joseph swirled the water with his stick. Maybe if the goats saw him touching it, they–

A flash of light echoed off the clear waters, a brilliant pulse coming from the far side of the riverbank. Joseph's heart leapt into his throat as, directly across the Jabbok, four kneeling figures rose.

The boy stumbled back a pace and fell flat on his rear in shock. The four armored men stood, pulling their mammoth blades from the ground and quietly sheathing them before turning to leave. In the pre-dawn light, the Messengers powerful glow from the night before seemed to have dimmed slightly, and their blades only shimmered instead of pulsing off a radiant fire.

Joseph's mouth hung open. Had they been there the whole time? How had he missed them? It was like they'd just appeared or...

For a stunned moment he watched as the Messengers hiked up the far bank, then vanished above it without a word. Joseph stood there, frozen, staring after the strange warriors.

Had the goats been able to see that?

That would explain why they'd been so keen on keeping their distance.

He was still wondering if he'd missed anything else when another figure appeared at the crest of the slope above the river. Joseph's eyes went wide, "Dad?"

Moving slower than usual, Dad limped his way down the slope to the opposite river bank. "Joseph?"

He seemed surprised, but not in a bad way, calling out as he waded into the current, "What are you doing here, son?"

"I..." That felt like an easy question, but in the moment Joseph couldn't put together the right words, "Ummm..."

Even limping, the splash of cold water seemed to motivate Dad. He quickly made it across, clapping the boy on the shoulder. "Well, I'm glad someone's already awake."

Dad's upbeat demeanor seemed like such a complete reversal from last night that it left Joseph feeling a little dizzy. Then it had seemed like the world was ending, with everyone frantically trying to cross the river in the pitch dark. Mom had been worried, Dad had straight up left, and they'd spent the night outside under blankets. Now, Dad was back and suddenly everything seemed fine except for...

"Are you alright?" Joseph stared at his father's new limping gait. It didn't seem to be slowing him down, but it was certainly enough to be noticeable.

Jacob hesitated, glancing at his leg. "It... it's fine. I just..."

Apparently, Dad couldn't decide what exactly he'd done and left the sentence hanging. Filled to the brim with curiosity, Joseph couldn't stop the next breathless question from slipping out. "What happened?"

His father hesitated, then opened his mouth like he was about to answer before closing it again. Finally, he settled on, "Ask me again in about ten years. When you're older."

"What?" Joseph's mouth dropped open, suddenly feeling cheated. "But that's like... ten years from now!"

"Clever boy," Dad joked, before looking up at something behind him, and nodding appreciatively. "I see you managed to keep the goats from scattering."

Joseph spun to discover the goats had finally decided the river was now suitably safe. While Dad had waded over, they must have edged their way down the slope until they were barely five paces behind him, warily staring at the two of them.

"Uhhh, yeah." Joseph waved his stick for the goats to go on by. Apparently they did speak *stick,* because in a moment, several rams had cautiously slid past the both of them, trotting down to the river side and greedily slurping up water.

Dad gave him an encouraging squeeze on the shoulder. "Come on," he nodded up the pebble strewn bank, now clearly visible in the gathering dawn, "The goats can manage on their own for a while."

Dad set off up the riverbank as the goats streamed by. In a moment, the two had crested the top, where they found themselves staring out across the scattered remnants of their previously ordered camp. Across the grassy plain, camels and people were scattered like so many pebbles. Off to the left, the cattle were just stirring from where they'd bedded down for the night. Meanwhile, the sheep were still curled up nearby, several hundred flecks of white strewn amid tall stalks of grass.

Behind the animals, the sun was rising. Joseph shielded his eyes as the fiery orb crested the horizon, the first rays of day flooding the plain.

Mom had her back to them, quietly folding up the blanket from the prior night as Dad limped up behind her. "Rachel?"

She jumped in shock and spun, the blanket spilling onto the grass as one hand covered her mouth. "Jacob," she whispered, breathless, "you're here."

"Of course," Dad grabbed her in a tight embrace, and Joseph looked away as they kissed, his face flushing. When they did break apart, there were tears in Mom's eyes.

"What happened?"

Dad shook his head, "We can talk later."

"DAD!" Two other familiar shouts echoed nearby, and Joseph looked up to see Issachar and Zebulun barrel across the field. They slammed into Dad so hard he nearly tumbled over. Dad laughed. "Boys," he held them both as the crowd around him steadily swelled. Reuben seemed to sum everything up when he wandered over with a confused, "Dad, where did you go?"

Dad didn't answer, just offered him a pat on the shoulder and a smile.

Everyone was still crowding in when their senior hunters, a lean, older Egyptian named Bariel and a younger Kaphtorian named Nashu, shouldered through the crowd. Bariel gave a curt nod. "Sir, they're here."

"They?" Jacob glanced up in confusion.

"Your brother," Bariel turned, pointing. To the south lay ranks of widely spaced low hills with broad valleys sprawled out between. They'd crossed the river onto a narrow plain, and snaking out from behind the nearest hill, Joseph glimpsed what could only be a column of men. For an instant, the conversation died as everyone turned to watch the approaching army. The soldiers must have kept to the low ground to avoid fighting through the scrub trees that capped the hillside. Now, even as they watched, Joseph saw the column curve straight towards them, barely more than a half hour's march away.

Chapter 4

Esau

When Joseph tore his eyes away from the approaching column, Bariel and his father were speaking in hushed voices. "They must have set out before dawn," Bariel said.

Dad nodded, even as a wave of worried whispers swept through his family. A hand grabbed Joseph, and he looked up as Mom pulled him tightly against her side.

Dad seemed almost miraculously calm though, especially when compared to yesterday. Then they'd been camped on the opposite bank when Bariel had found him, Mom and Dad in Dad's tent. Dad and Bariel had both stepped outside, conversing in hushed tones, while Mom had tried to distract him. He'd still caught a few words though, *Esau* and *army*. When Dad had stepped back inside, the change was almost frightening. He looked like he'd aged another ten years in just those few minutes.

Today though, Dad radiated confidence. He took in the situation at a glance. It was... bad. Even Joseph could tell that. Bariel spoke up. "Should we try and retreat back across the river? I can tell Kerlan to..."

"Don't bother," Dad held up a hand to interrupt. "We'll stay on this side. Have the herdsmen round up any stragglers and ensure the animals don't scatter. Have everyone else wait here. Make sure they eat and all the animals are watered."

"But, sir..."

Bariel opened his mouth to protest, but Jacob cut him off. "I'll see to my brother."

The lead hunter hesitated an instant, clearly searching for a counterpoint. Finally, he nodded with a slight bow, "Of course."

"Excellent." By now the entire family had gathered– all of Joseph's brothers, Leah and Dinah, Bilhah and Zilpah, and of course Mom. All uhh... Joseph had to do a quick count, and he almost ran out of fingers... twice... all seventeen of them.

Dad looked around, pulled in a deep breath, then declared, "I need the rest of you to come with me. I believe the polite thing is to go greet my brother. I'm sure he'll want to meet you all."

Mom didn't say a word, but Joseph still felt her tense, and heard her sharp inhalation at the pronouncement. Across from them, Leah's mouth dropped open like he'd just suggested they all go enjoy some nightshade berries. "Jacob, we can't just walk up to—"

"We *can*, actually," Jacob remarked dryly. "I believe that's the usual way of greeting family."

Leah's voice turned icy, "And if your brother is still...?"

She let the sentence hang and Joseph swallowed, wishing someone would just explain what was going on for a change. If Uncle Esau was still... *what*? Obviously, it was bad. But Dad wouldn't talk about it, Mom just changed the subject when he asked, and he doubted his brothers knew either.

A few nights ago, during the trip from Harran, Levi had given his explanation in serious words around the campfire. In his story, Dad and Uncle Esau had once been best friends. That was, until one day when they'd been out in the fields and found this beautiful girl just alone in the grass. She'd needed help, so they'd taken her back to their camp, where they'd both instantly fallen in love with her, and...

Joseph wasn't exactly sure what had happened next. He'd stopped listening. That said, he was *mostly* certain Levi was making everything up to sound smart. That felt like a very Levi sort of thing.

But then again, if Levi's version was wrong, then why was Uncle Esau coming with so many men? And why was everyone so worried?

Joseph wished he'd done a bit *more* spying when Mom and Dad were talking. Even if he wasn't supposed to.

Before anyone else could object, Dad declared bluntly, "We're going to meet them."

Leah's expression drew tight, and Joseph wasn't sure if she was angry or scared. "Even if that means your brother—"

"Yes," Dad cut her off. "Leah, we're on the wrong side of the river, no matter what we do. Might as well make the best of it."

Leah looked like she might make more of a fuss, but Dad cut her off with a gesture, "Bilhah, Zilpah, I want you two and your boys to follow first. Then you, Leah. Rachel will come last. I'll go on ahead. If something happens..." he hesitated, "do what seems best." He looked like he might say something more, then sighed and nodded, "Come on."

Five minutes later, Joseph dug in his heels and tugged at Mom's hand, trying to drag her to the side as they followed a few dozen paces behind Leah and the rest of his brothers. "Why do we have to be in the back?" he complained. "I can't see anything."

"Joseph, STOP!" Mom's voice had a whip-crack sting, and she jerked his arm hard to pull him back next to her.

"Oww." Joseph rubbed his shoulder and glanced up at her in surprise, suddenly wary. He just wanted to see what was going on. Was Dad okay? Why was it that everyone else got to act so worried, but he was expected to just sit here where all he could see was Reuben's rear and relax?

After Dad had barked out all his orders and set off towards the oncoming column, Mom and Leah had broken out in one of their little *whisper wars*. It had ended with Leah stalking off, fuming, while Mom had strode back to him wearing an anxious frown. Mom was acting like they'd gotten the better end of the deal, except Joseph didn't see what the logic was putting the shortest person dead last in line.

Up ahead, Leah's group abruptly stopped and Mom followed suit. Her hold on his hand tightened. Joseph looked up to see her nibbling at her lower lip, eyes staring far past Leah.

Something was happening, and stuck down where he might as well have been blind, the anticipation was killing him. For a moment, Joseph sullenly scraped his sandal against a clump of grass that barely went up to his knee. It kicked it several times, slowly tearing the base out of the bronzed dirt. Finally, the clump sagged outwards into a messy green mop that looked like Simeon's hair when he forgot to wet it in the morning—

"Joseph," Mom's tone sliced the air like a razor. He glanced up to see his mother stiffly glowering down at him.

What? He wasn't doing anything wrong. It was just grass. He gave the loose clump a cautious nudge, and Mom let out a hiss of a sigh. "Fine." She nodded over to the side. "You can look, *but*," her gaze narrowed, sharp enough to make him gulp, "You stay close and get back here when I tell you."

"Yeah," he nodded, eagerly. "Okay."

Mom shook her head, but released his hand. Joseph jogged five paces to the left, angling so he could get a good view.

What he saw was an oncoming snake of spear-toting warriors. And there were *a lot* of them, hundreds. Back in Harran, he'd seen a couple of the larger caravans tromping their way towards the city. Dad would sell them goats and sheep to eat. They could be huge, thirty guards scattered among several hundred donkeys that were all roped together into sprawling trains.

Uncle Esau though, he was coming with a huge army, the men marching in a loose file and stunningly well-armed. Now that they were closer, Joseph could catch glints off their spearpoints, and the distinctive curves of strung bows. A few soldiers even carried giant battle clubs studded with razor flint shards that looked like they could tear him in two with just a swing. In the lead strode a giant of a man. He wore a marvelous coat of polished bronze scales that clung to his body like a golden second skin.

And way out in front of them all, Joseph saw Dad walking towards the army... alone, no weapons, no armor, no army beside him. In that instant, the pieces suddenly clicked into place, and it made perfect sense why everyone was so afraid. Joseph swallowed a hard lump in his throat as his dad paused and bowed.

It was the deep, bend-at-the-waist sort of bow he reserved for important visitors– mainly caravan leaders who came to trade and Uncle Laban when Dad was feeling formal.

As Joseph watched though, Dad proceeded to take a few steps and bow again.... and again... and again as Uncle Esau approached. Joseph blinked, silently counting as Dad bowed– *seven* times?

That was the sort of thing that they'd do if... well, Joseph didn't know. *Maybe* if they'd been given an audience with King Rihat of Harran. Maybe.

As Dad finished, the front figure broke away from the advancing column. Spear in hand, the man charged towards Jacob.

Joseph felt a horrible stab of fear as the figure struck Dad and...

The two embraced?

"Joseph," Mom called. He tore his eyes away to see her gesturing him back. He cast one last glance to see that Dad was alright and caught the giant man's spear dropping discarded into the grass beside them. Then he jogged over to ask, "What's happening?"

Mom was still standing stiffly at attention, but her grip seemed softer as she took his hand. "I don't know." She peered ahead another moment, then abruptly knelt down in front of him, smoothing out his hair and picking a stray bit of sticky weed off his tunic. "Alright," she said in a hushed tone, "when we meet your uncle, I want you to stand up straight, then give a proper bow. Don't pester him with questions, just be polite, and stay near me."

Joseph glanced ahead to where Leah was also busy scolding her boys into a semblance of a line. "So then, we'll get to meet—"

"Yes, now quiet," Mom said. She hurriedly straightened his grubby tunic, then stepped back a moment, cocking her head to one side and regarding him with a skeptical frown. Eventually she sighed with a mumbled, "Well, that'll have to do," and shook her head.

She spent another hurried moment brushing the dust from her own skirt, and up ahead Joseph saw the rest of his brothers start walking. Mom smoothed her raven black hair, then took his hand with a deep breath. "Let's go."

Unfortunately, Joseph still couldn't see anything. Trailing after all his brothers, he followed until suddenly everyone in front stopped and abruptly bowed low as well. He got his first real glimpse of Uncle Esau past them, and the man was *huge*. Like, Dad was big, but not compared to his brother. Honestly, Joseph didn't see the family resemblance at all.

Then all his brothers rose, and he had to wait there a moment, scuffing at the dirt and puffing out his cheeks while everyone else got to walk on ahead. He was just wondering how long they were going to have to wait, when suddenly everyone else shuffled aside. He and Mom were facing Uncle Esau with Dad standing to one side, gesturing them up.

"Come on, Joseph." Mom led him forward. The two paused before Father and Uncle Esau and Joseph gave his best attempt at a formal bow.

"This is my wife, Rachel," Dad introduced them, "and my son, Joseph."

Joseph wasn't sure how long he was supposed to bow. There was probably some rule about it that no one had bothered to tell him. He counted until three and looked up to see his uncle nodding to them in return.

Mom dipped her head and bobbed in a curtsey, "An honor to meet you, my lord."

Esau seemed much more polite than Joseph would have expected. "The honor is all mine."

Esau stepped forward, suddenly towering dizzyingly tall over Joseph. "And you," he boomed. Strong hands grabbed Joseph around the waist, and suddenly the young boy was smoothly hoisted skywards. He found himself face to face with a smiling, hairy giant. "You're a little one."

He gulped, "H... Hello... sir."

Esau seemed to think that was particularly funny and burst into deep chuckles. The man gently lowered Joseph back down, patted him on the head, then nodded to Jacob. "And what were all the flocks and herds I met as I came?"

Dad shifted slightly on his feet, and for an instant Joseph could swear he seemed almost embarrassed. "They are a gift, my lord, to ensure your friendship."

Esau shook his head. "I already have plenty, my brother. Keep what you have for yourself."

Dad actually seemed taken aback that he'd been declined. "No, if I have found favor with you please accept this gift from me. And what a relief to see your friendly smile. It is like seeing the face of God."

The two kept talking, but Joseph was only half listening. Instead, he focused on Uncle Esau's armor. On his head, the man wore a simple peaked bronze cap with a chinstrap. But his armor... it was magnificent, a heavy piece of leather studded with reinforced bronze circles polished to a mirror finish.

Except for the Messengers and their unique armament, Joseph had only ever seen the boiled leather armor of caravan guards and the few pieces in Father's own small collection. Father's armory mostly consisted of functional boiled leather with little decoration. But Uncle Esau's bronze armor far eclipsed anything his family had, elegant and menacing in the same breath.

He and Dad were busy discussing the herds they'd sent ahead, Dad insisting until Uncle Esau finally relented and accepted the gift.

For a while the two just talked. Joseph only half paid attention as he slowly scuffed a nice symmetric hole in the ground with his sandal. His ears perked up though when they had a spare moment to ask questions. Reuben finally got up the guts to ask the one they'd all been wondering, *how had Uncle Esau gotten his armor*? Just buying a piece like that would have been ruinously expensive.

Leah glared at him with an exasperated, "Reuben, can't you—"

"It's quite okay," Uncle Esau grinned at the wide-eyed stares. "You boys can touch it if you'd like. I'll be having the servants oil it when I get back regardless."

Almost at once, several of the boys crowded around, Joseph included, even though he caught his mom's exasperated sigh. He just ignored her. When else would they get to see something like this up close? He even managed to slide in and touch one of the plates. It was cool to his fingers and wonderfully smooth.

"Where did you get it?" Levi asked, with rapt curiosity.

"I took it off a raiding party from Ashkelon," Esau declared. "We ambushed them after they'd burned a village and their leader challenged me to a duel. Obviously, I accepted." He pointed to a deep dent on a plate near his waist where the bronze had been badly scored. "This was where I missed him. You can see how tough it was. It deflected my spear and he nearly ran me though, except that..."

Uncle Esau's voice trailed off, leaving them all hanging in anticipation. "It's a long story," the burly man said. "How about I tell you more tonight?" He looked over to Father, "It's still morning. Let's move on, and I'll go ahead of you. You can never tell who might by lying in ambush in these valleys."

Dad hesitated. "I'm not sure that's possible. We've already come a very long way just to arrive here."

Esau waved to brush away the objection, "It's still early, brother. We have the whole day before us."

"Yes, but what of my children?" Jacob gestured with a sweeping open palm to all of them. "You can see, my lord, that some of the children are very young, And the flocks and herds have their young too." Dad seemed to be nodding in Joseph's general direction and the boy sighed. He wasn't *that* young.

"If they are driven too hard, even for one day, all the animals could die. Please, my lord, go on ahead of your servant. We will follow slowly, at a pace that is comfortable for the livestock and the children. I will meet you in Seir."

For the first time since Joseph had met him, Uncle Esau hesitated, slowly nodding to himself. Finally, he said, "Very well, but at least let me assign some of my men to guide and protect you."

Dad shook his head. "That's not necessary. It's enough that you've received me warmly, my lord."

Uncle Esau looked past them for a moment, taking in the animals strung out between them and the river. "You're certain, brother?"

Jacob nodded, "We've come all the way from Harran, I'm certain we can make it a little further on our own."

Esau nodded, then abruptly embraced Jacob in a fierce hug, clapping him on the back. "Very well, brother." Joseph caught tears in both Esau's and his dad's eyes.

Esau stepped back, taking them all in. "I'm glad you've returned, and I look forward to seeing you again." He nodded to the rest of them, with a wide grin, "All of you."

"The next time we meet, I'll introduce you to *my* boys." Esau stepped in and clapped Reuben on the shoulder, giving Joseph the rare pleasure of seeing his oldest brother gulp in alarm under the attention of the powerfully built warrior. "And I'll tell you more about the *previous* owner of this armor," he tapped at his chest.

Turning, his uncle reached down and plucked his spear out of the grass, where none of them had dared touch it. Twirling it in a salute, he added, "If we do find anyone on the road back, I'll make sure to chase them *very* far away." From his wolffish grin, Joseph could tell Uncle Esau wasn't exaggerating.

The man walked back towards his soldiers, signaling with his spear. In just a few moments the column had turned, with Esau in the lead, guiding them back to Mount Seir.

Jacob watched them go. As they left, the servants Father had sent yesterday to escort his *gift* to Uncle Esau, broke away from the column. They headed back for their own group, making for his father, who promptly ordered them to rejoin the rest of their mess of a camp. Finally, his uncle had vanished around the slope of the nearest hill, and Dad turned back to the rest of them, grinning like a madman. "I'd say that went well."

"Surprisingly so," Leah agreed with a note of relief.

"He seemed like a nice man." Rachel remarked, cheekily, "I think you do him a disservice."

"Perhaps," Jacob sighed. "He's definitely changed… I suppose we've both changed."

He looked back towards the scattered herds. Joseph could see the servants slowly trying to reassemble some sense of order after their frantic late-night crossing.

"Now, I think we've all had enough excitement for today," Jacob said. As though merely the mention had reminded him of last night, he raised one hand to cover a yawn. "How about we check on the animals, put up a few tents, then take the rest of the day off?" His eyes swept across them all. "Does that sound good?"

It sounded *aaaamazing*. Joseph let out a relieved breath. Together the rest of his family turned to go as Dad added, "Welcome home, everyone."

TO BE CONTINUED IN
<u>THE DAYS OF JOSEPH</u>

Afterword

Hopefully you enjoyed *The Days of Joseph, Mahaniam.* This is a fairly short narrative, but no doubt you're already aware that Joseph has a much longer journey ahead of him. If you're interested in more of Joseph's biblical adventures, I'd suggest you check out the next book in this saga simply titled <u>*The Days of Joseph*</u>.

Since this is a short story, I'll be brief and simply explain that I've tried to stick as close to the original story as possible. Where available, I've kept the dialogue pulled directly from the text and tried not to take too many creative liberties. As always though, with these sorts of projects, there is a lot of filling in the blanks. And I'm quite cognizant that I've made a few creative choices with this short story that probably require explanation.

I'll start by simply pointing out that, if you read Genesis 32 and 33 literally, there are some truly strange things going on. First, as I've tried to highlight in the story, Jacob's decision to cross the Jabbok River in the middle of the night is absolutely bizarre.

I spent much of my youth ranching with my own dad, and as a general rule, you *do not* move animals at night… particularly across water.

Most animals are hesitant enough about being pushed across pitifully small creeks during the day. Doing that at night is basically asking for a disaster.

As someone who'd spent twenty years herding animals, Jacob would have known this. And while we often skim over this note today without much consideration, to farmers and herders in the ancient world, the detail would have stood out instantly. The fact that Jacob chose to cross a stream into a markedly inferior tactical position *in the dark* makes the tale even more unusual.

Either, Jacob woke up in the middle of the night and completely lost his mind, or there was something else going on. Hence the angels surrounding his camp. We know there was an encampment of angels somewhere nearby since it's mentioned in Genesis 32:1. Although, in the spirit of full disclosure, the word translated as angels is actually messengers (this is typical throughout the Old Testament). So, this scene *can* simply be read as noting that some *messengers* showed up with some sort of welcome news. But that also makes it odd that Jacob would call the place where it happened, the Camp of God.

Regardless, I've taken the view that Jacob ran into actual angels, which I feel is justified given that God Himself shows up later in the story. The angels surrounding his camp in the night, isn't anything I can provide direct scriptural evidence for, but it *is* the only reason I can think why Jacob would attempt something so foolhardy. He might have had a worrying dream or premonition, but usually that would get a mention in the text, as it does in Genesis 31:24. In short, something happened to leave Jacob seriously panicked, but we don't know what precisely, so this is my attempt at an educated guess.

I should also mention that I wasn't entirely sure what to do with Jacob splitting his camp into two groups in Genesis 32:7. Given that both camps would have had to cross the ford, they can't have been located very far apart. And since all of Jacob's children and wives show up to greet Esau, the two camps must have been operating very closely. This split may simply have been administrative. Jacob might have appointed a deputy over a subgroup of herdsmen and animals so that, if he was pressed, his household could retreat in multiple directions. Regardless, it doesn't seem to have affected the story on a practical level, so I didn't make any real mention of it.

Finally, if you're reading the text very closely, you might have seen that most translations of Genesis 32:22-23 simply say that Jacob sent over his family and possessions. There's no mention of him crossing with them, then immediately heading back. However, practically speaking, this sort of frantic, late-night move would have required a great deal of close supervision. After dwelling on the question for quite some time, I concluded it wasn't a stretch to posit that Jacob might have at least gotten his feet wet seeing everyone across.

At the end of the day, please understand that these are just my views, and you're obviously free to disagree. But please also know that I did actually consider these questions, and this story is simply my way or resolving many of them.

With all that said however, I hope you enjoyed the story. If you're interested in other, much wilder adventures of Biblical characters, including the story of an older and more mature Joseph, I'd encourage you to check out my other books.

Joseph – The Days of Joseph

Elijah – The Days of Elijah

And if you need to contact me:
My email - johntheauthor1@gmail.com

Citations

Ancient Hebrew doesn't have quotation marks, and dialogue was routinely paraphrased. That said, I used exact dialogue from the Book of Genesis where translators provided it. I mixed and matched Bible versions to find the translation I feel flows best within the rest of the narrative and most closely matches my own writing style.

Below are the biblical references for the book. The Chapter in *this book* where the citation is used is listed first and the biblical chapter and verse numbers are listed second. The appropriate version citations are shown last. If you have ten minutes, I'd encourage you to check out the source material, as it's pretty readily available. Note: full verses are often cited, but only the dialogue is actually quoted.

1. Chapter 3: Genesis 32:2 (NLT)
2. Chapter 4: Genesis 33:8 (NLT)
3. Chapter 4: Genesis 33:9 (NIV)
4. Chapter 4: Genesis 33:10 (NLT)
5. Chapter 4: Genesis 33:12 (HCSB)
6. Chapter 4: Genesis 33:13-15 (NLT)